Unsold Virgin

By

Naveen Miriyala

Copyright © 2025 by Naveen Miriyala

All rights reserved.

This book or any portion thereof may not be reproduced or used in any manner whatsoever without the express written permission of the respective author of the respective story, except for the use of brief quotations in a book review.

The writer of the respective work holds sole responsibility for the originality of the content and IndiePress is not responsible in any way whatsoever.

Printed in India

IndiePress

ISBN: 978-93-7197-659-6

First Printing, 2025

IndiePress

A division of Nasadiya Technologies Private Ltd.

Koramangala, Bengaluru

Karnataka-560029

http://indiepress.in/

Typeset by MAP Systems, Bengaluru

Book Cover designed by Nikhil Kamath

Publishing Consultant: Rechal Fernandes

THANK YOU NOTE

I, Naveen Miriyala, who buried my old passion, planned my career in the Corporate Sector, and accordingly created a plan to reach heights. But randomly, I met a friend who is already a beautiful writer and a poet. When we were working together, one day during our lunchtime, along with other friends, we discussed movies, writing, and stories. That was the day I found out she is a writer. All of a sudden, a buried thought from my memory pops up, and I express to her that I also wanted to become a Writer and Director once. That was the moment she gently nudged me toward introducing me to an app where stories could be poured straight from the heart.

I gave it a thought for two days and decided to give it a try to avoid feeling regret in the future. And this is what happened after that decision. I always wanted to thank her, but in a beautiful way. I believe that my first book will be the best one to express my gratitude for waking up my old dream and finding a new talent along with a corporate future.

We don't always know why certain conversations happen, but the universe does. That lunch break wasn't just about food it served me a side of purpose. I revealed my old glitch to become a writer and director, which I had left behind. Unknowingly, I'm here today, who wrote a book that I never expected. I wrote this book with pure intentions and passion for writing. So, I would love to thank my friend with every letter and space of this book.

From the start of my writing to now and the future, every letter that I write will always thank my friend without a second thought.

Thank you, Dhanya R

by

Every letter from Naveen Miriyala

THANK YOU NOTE

After a nearly 3-year sincere trails, got few responses but unfortunately negative. I was in a position where a lot of confusion takes place whether to continue writing or focus on career by leaving writing. It was an uncontrollable emotion because I don't want to leave writing but I took my career little lighter by focusing on writing.

One day, in an interview, a question by Mrs Anupama Chopra, Film Companion to Rajamouli Sir, where multiple giants like Mr Kamal Haasan, Ms Priyanka Dutt, Mr Gautham Menon, Mr Prithvi Raj, and Mr Lokesh Kanagraj were present in that interview. As a last question in the interview, Mrs Anupama Chopra asked, "What kind of changes you people wanted to see for coming decade in the Film Industry?"

Rajamouli Sir answered, "Once upon a time in India, we had a beautiful writers where every producer, actor, director, technician wanted to work on their stories but now industry is lacking such kind of writers. I personally wanted to see such writers again in the industry where everyone waits for his dates to be part on their stories". That one answer hit my thoughts and stayed with me.

This is the answer that struck back in mind at that particular moment. There is one dialogue by our Trivikram sir in "Aravinda Sametha Veera Raghava" movie, "The value and worth of any suggestion will change its impact depends on person saying and time (our situation)".

UNSOLD VIRGIN

I don't know whether I will become a successful writer or this book is going to reach many readers but that one line said by Rajamouli Sir hits me very hard and stayed with me, eventually which motivated me to work on both paths Corporate and Writing in parallel until I got a chance and success.

After that decision, 'Unsold Virgin' happened in the process of trails to become as a writer. I am always inspired not by Rajamouli Sir' movies but by his BTS hard work and passion for film making. Thank you Sir for Inspiring me and us. You are Freedom fighter of Indian Film Industry (IFI) who united whole India once again without any thoughts.

Thank you, Rajamouli Sir

by

Every letter from Naveen Miriyala

a small story about feelings and mindset

ACKNOWLEDGMENT

THANK YOU, SOCIETY!

CONTENTS

Preface xiii

Introduction xv

Birth 1

Childhood 2

'First' Moment 6

First Encounter 13

Real Meaning 22

Knowing Society 44

Back to Home 54

PREFACE

SEX-HUNGER-SLEEP or SLEEP-SEX-HUNGER or HUNGER-SLEEP-SEX

The above order is always a mystery in society. I don't know the order in the inception stage or how the creators planned it. In a cycle chain process, it is always very difficult to explain which is first unless they are creators. But you know, these are the only three things created by creators to continue their living for all species. After the deadly evolution of the human species, invented a lot of things in society are in the name of culture. Even though after millions of years of evolution, no one knows who is the ruler of the jungle, whether a male or female in the early period. And at times, the feelings and emotions of the human race have evolved better than any other species on Earth. Due to the rapid increase in the Human race, different morals have been inserted into different feelings and emotions according to their comfort.

Maybe this story can't be able to explain all kinds of emotions or feelings but surely discusses the feelings and emotions that are related to the word "Virgin". This story travels through the life of a sex worker named "Prashna", who is one of the girls from the House of Prostitution, and understands the meaning of the word Virgin from society in a different perspective and knows the usage of the word Virgin in specific things. She always wondered about this word and why it is not considered for everything. Finally, her life journey explains whether she understands the real meaning or is lost to the societal meaning of the word "VIRGIN".

INTRODUCTION

In the darkest closed bedroom where sunlight is penetrating through a hole in the broken window, a woman is making sounds moaning with pain. A man is stroking very hard as that is his last time. He is in his late thirties and comes from an orthodox family. And the moment came when he reached his peak and started making sounds. And there it is, he's done. After a few seconds, he pushed the woman aside and lay on the bed. "Today I enjoyed it a lot", he said. He then sits and watches the woman on the bed with an expression of achievement. Pulled his shirt from the table which is closely attached to the bed. Takes out the money and gives it to the woman. Wears his shirt walks out from the room and does not turn his back even once. She stayed on the bed for a minute. Her facial expressions showed that she was controlling her pain and trying to regain normal. Finally, she got some energy and got out of the bed. Arranged her saree to normal.

And that woman is me, Prashna, who was born and raised in the House of Prostitution. Yes, you are correct. I'm a Prostitute. And this is my story. I always wanted to have a friend and discuss all my problems but unfortunately didn't find one. So, I am eager and enthusiastic to share my life with all the readers.

Wait, before diving into my story I just wanted to share a few thoughts that can give a small introduction to how I think.

UNSOLD VIRGIN

Every day as the sunlight gently approaches and kisses the ice in the Himalayas like a morning routine, that gentle touch makes the ice feel like her man is taking care of his lovely woman with deep love and making her slowly melt down to the purest droplets of water as their baby. As a newborn baby playfully slips from its mother's lap, the droplets of water playfully slip from its mother's lap. As she is the daughter of the Sun whose rays travel with light speed, the baby travels with the same speed from the lap of her mother to the feet where it touches the land. The irony is here until the daughter water touches the dirty land, water is the purest and cleanest ever in her life. When it touches the dirty land, the innocence and purity of water are gone. Looks like she is a mix of both now. From there the travel becomes very difficult to the water. In every inch of steps in her path, she collects the waste and mixes it with her purity. When the water hits the hurdles, she feels a huge pain which forces her to take another path where the waste is more to collect in her way. Likewise, she becomes dirty by erasing her purity on the way and finally reaches the destination called Ocean which is a hell of impurity as there is no other way. This is a continuous life cycle process for her. It always reminds me of one line.

Birth Is Clean, Death Is Dirty

BIRTH

In the world of never-ending battles between eight legs, generations are created for the greater good. But unfortunately, not for all. One day a baby girl was born beside the battlefield when the war was continuing where the sun never rises to throw a light. A mother is happy for the baby. In Indian stories, people do a festival at home when a girl is born but they are limited to stories only. In reality, not everyone does the same because it all depends on the status of the family. My family falls under the category where people start seeing the girl as a product that can create a high value in the market coming few years. The girl was me and they had given me the name Sukhi (which means 'pleasure' in one of the Indian languages). But later because of the number of questions I used to ask, they teased me with a name called 'Prashna' (the question) which eventually became my name.

CHILDHOOD

I always wonder what babies think in their minds when they don't know they are kids. In my childhood when my mother keeps me in the swing to make sleep, maybe I always wonder how and why the entire building is created to hold this swing. Why did my mother spend all the money on creating this huge building to hold the swing? Mother is crazy for me. After giving it a such thought-provoking thought I used to go to sleep.

Every war will end one day, but these wars in our house are never-ending. My age was around 7-8 years now, wars are still happening. We as kids all started to get to know little about the world through by playing games, watching movies, roaming around our houses, etc. Likewise, one day I went to the vegetable market along with my mother. Ever in my lifetime, that was the first time I saw people running like hell on the streets. Firstly, I was afraid of them and held my mother's hand very tightly. She patted me and controlled my fear by taking me closer to her. After a few minutes, the crowd was normal and I asked my mother what it was about. My mother replied, "When any hero comes on the streets people run like this to see them". Then I said, "Oh, in that case, we are also celebrities, right? Because every day so many people come to our houses". My mother laughed at my innocence.

Maybe that was the age for everyone where they were very innocent and filled with many questions. I'm also one of them. I used to irritate my mother with a lot of questions every day. If I'm not a girl, then my mother could have thrown me away.

I used to ask a lot of questions like Who made this world? Who is God? Is God real? Why were there day & night? When will God come to our home? Why in our families all were women? Why are different men coming to our houses every day? Some are new and few regular. Who is my father? Where is my father? When is he coming back to us? These are the most common questions I used to ask but most depend on the situation.

My mother never told me the answers to those questions even when she knew them. But one question always hits me even now like an asteroid hit the Earth which shatters the planet. That is "Who is my father?

Before that let me tell you how my mother got into here. Those were the no-worry days in life, around the age of 5 years, my grandmother told my mother to not go outside to play. Until kids are in the hands of parents, they are safe, once the control of parents is gone then that will be the end. That day my mother cried and stepped down from her mother's lap and ran outside to play. In the kitchen, milk was making the sound of running out from the safest place due to heat generated by flames of broken wooden pieces. Grandmother runs to stop the milk's self-sacrifice. My mother got the chance and ran onto the road outside our house which is the path to the world outside. In a thunder-lightening moment, two guys on the cycle came and took my mother away with them. They kidnapped my mother. Sold her here in this market. This was the journey of my mother to this place.

Now come back to my story. As like everyone's childhood mine is also going smoother. Playing with other kids near our street, watching movies, living in our worlds. Never bothered about the things happening around out there in the world. Our parents didn't like to send us to education schools. And of course, schools are not ready to teach us. There are so many things out there we never heard of them.

For example, never encountered the word economy in our lives because we never bothered about where it is used and why. We feel like earning money to complete a day is big and far enough for us. That's how our mindsets are prepared.

One day with our street kids went to the playground that we used to go to regularly in high school. That day there were barriers boards and not allowing all the kids because a small function was going on like a ceremony for kids' achievements. Parents came along with the kids.

Every kid was speaking in a language that we never heard in our lives till then. Felt like they are from another country. But later got to know that the language is English. They were very much fluent in speaking.

"I would like to thank my parents for always supporting me", one kid said.

"I am always grateful to have such a wonderful family", another kid said.

"I love my parents and teachers for their support", another kid.

"For everyone who motivated and helped me, thank you, Love you Mom and Dad", another kid.

Everyone is clapping after every kid spoke. I have seen happiness on the kid's faces as well as on their parents.

I felt bad after seeing them. It hurts.

"Why did our parents never send us to school?" I questioned myself. But never found an answer.

On my way back home, I thought of asking my mother to go to school. Like every child, I wanted to be praised for my achievements. When those parents praised their kids, I felt very happy. But I know my mother's answer.

That is a big NO.

I never understand my mother's intentions as a kid. She always stops me from doing so many things like other kids are doing. She never allowed me much time to play, never sent me to school, after 6 P.M. didn't allow me to be outside, sometimes she used to sit very silent. Maybe because of my age and maturity, I always understood that the depth of water is the same in the bucket and the Ocean. I hope one day I can find all the answers to my questions.

Childhood is Innocence

'FIRST' MOMENT

First Cry

First Food

First Steps

First Bath

First Words

First Achievement

First Salary

First Marriage

First Wife

First Kiss

First Child

First Sleep

Every first is very special in anyone's life because they'll never be able to feel the same first again in their entire life. But for females, there is one thing in their life that changes them from girl to woman when they get their First Period.

First Period.

A droplet of water steps down from the lap of mother iceberg travels through the hurdles in her life and joins a big pond.

At this moment, our owner is happier than my mother.

Yes! Real life begins for me.

Our owner is so happy on my first period because there is a higher value for me in the market. Customers always look for new and fresh things even though when it comes to humans but the irony is they are not.

After a year, our owner starts finding big fish in the market to get big money. It is very easy to find a big fish in this line, for one job there are lakhs of people who are ready to do it.

My owner is an expert in picking up the person who can pay more and more for such. Her life started here and later started her business line. Has many contacts and names & fame in the market. She can pick the right vegetables at the right time in the market.

In this line of business, they kept the customers waiting to increase their enthusiasm.

More demand. More value.

After all the excitement that surrounded me, I got afraid and went to my mother and said, "Maa I don't want to do this, I am afraid".

"Don't worry, I am also afraid for the first time", Mother replied.

I said, "Maa, please".

She didn't listen to me and said, "Don't worry, everything will be alright".

She left from there. She was an emotionless and iron-hearted person.

UNSOLD VIRGIN

I never told you about my mother's character right?

She is also a woman like others out there in society who has a dreamy world of having a nice family, cooking for her favorite people, wants to play with her children, takes care of her parents, deeply committed to achieving something in her life. But her life was unfortunate. A big turn has been taken at her early age where she doesn't even know about the world. She didn't shout when the kidnappers were holding her and escaping. Maybe she thought they were playing with her. She never knew that it was the last time she of smile happily and see her mother. From then, Darkness invited her with warm hands and showed how much the world was bigger in the darkness than in the light. In her initial days in the world of darkness, she searched for her light(mother) and cried daily. But she realized that light was never be able to found in the darkness. She accepted her fate. She never had any respect from the customers. Everyone treats her like a slave and is tortured very badly. She became cold and rock-solid at heart. Slowly became money-minded because of situations that surrounded her.

Heartless.

I sat silent for a few days. A huge fight was happening in me about why my mother was not listening to me. Why is she so stubborn?

Fear occupied me.

I don't know how can I explain my thoughts right then because I'm in a position where I was unable to express unexplainable fears running throughout the day. People were around in the broad daylight but still felt alone.

The day was arriving.

I still don't know how to deal with the situation. Mother and Owner are very much excited for the moment.

So many thoughts, how he was? How does he look? What was his age? Was he married or not? How he treats me? What will he do with me? Was he a good man or a bad man?

The day comes.

From the morning, everything is in a hurry and they are getting me ready for the moment.

I was Silent.

They were very much excited more than me because that day they would get more money than regular.

Times ticking near.

I don't have any words even in my imagination. Fear occupies all the space. Or I was unable to search the words in the darkness due to a lack of light inside the brain.

Customer came.

I was able to listen to them outside.

"Is she ready?", he asks.

"Yes, she is always ready for you", the owner replied.

He pushed the door and entered into the room.

I was sitting on the bed and my head was looking down with fear.

"Don't be shy", he said with a base voice which made me afraid.

After listening to the voice, my brain stopped working for a second and my hands started shivering slightly.

Because of my anxiety and fear, I was unable to recognize his face. Even I was not able to understand his words.

He was removing his clothes. Has this long gold chain which was very thick on his neck. Along with that, there are other two chains that are thin and in different lengths. A gold bangle with the right hand. Four rings for right-hand and left-hand fingers.

He started approaching me with a smile and hunger.

All of a sudden he touched my hand which made me nearly black out but awake. Hold my hand with a grip and ask me to be normal.

Till then, in my entire life, I have never felt that kind of harsh touch. I always had soft and gentle touches from surrounding people. I still believe that the world is so welcoming for a kind of kid like me. I used to see and grow many men coming to our houses but never understood why. I thought we were a kind of celebrity till that day.

The man came forward and whispered, "Don't be afraid, you are lucky".

My eyes are still closed.

He held my foot and pulled me.

Made me lay on the bed.

The smell from his was intolerable and gave me vomiting sensations.

He was on me now. I can't be able to take his unbearable weight.

The moment when he started, I felt that pain that was uncontrollable for me and started crying.

Still, he didn't stop.

His hunger was eternal.

Why I used 'eternal' is that man has no boundaries and limits. He never felt any concern after seeing me at that young age. Maybe this is cruelty.

After the end of the war between the elephant and the ant, the elephant left.

With pain, I was in bed and silently looking up to the roof.

I don't know how to explain the situation and pain I have gone through mentally, physically, and emotionally.

But I can say this, you may understand.

Have you ever thought about the soldiers with their broken bodies in a war from the losing side?

Those are the soldiers who have given everything for their King and lost their lives in fighting against the enemies of King due to his greed for land, money, and girls. No one understands the real pain of those lost soldiers after the war who always suffer for their broken bodies and families.

Feel their pain in the war field after the king got defeated and lost to the opposite king who left the field with pride. The bodies are everywhere on the field from the winning side and losing side. But for the winning side, at least they had their winning emotion along with their broken bodies. For the losing side, their bodies are left on the field after the war, waiting for someone to rescue but ends in losing hope. They need to get up on their own helping their teammates to get up and leave the place.

I believe a lost soldier always has thoughts like, "It is not our battle, it is not our greed, it gives nothing to us but pain, suffering, mourning for life, watching his family helpless, and they will never get their life back to normal.

Get back to my story.

After a few minutes, I came into consciousness and tried to move. It was very difficult to move after a huge pressure. One who experienced knows it well.

UNSOLD VIRGIN

Somehow managed to get up and sit on the bed.

Minutes later my mother came inside the room.

Sat beside me and laid her hand on my shoulder.

"I know what you are going through and how much pain you have", she said.

I feel she doesn't. She was one of the cruellest people to me at that moment.

"Don't worry, pain makes you stronger", she said and left.

And that was the day I got to understand why so many men visited our houses regularly. We are not celebrities; we are hunger healers.

Unknown battles with Unknown Warriors. Pain is inevitable.

FIRST ENCOUNTER

In the continuous flow of life, customers increased. The pain was addictive. Still doesn't know how to explain the pain. Got to know so many things slowly which are there in society. I understood that in my way.

Different people, different mentalities, different perspectives, different characters, different meanings, different ideologies, different explanations, different truths, different lies, different lives, different comforts, different motives, different good, different bad, different morals, different ethics, different judgements, different genders, different relations, different love, different levels of maturity, different understandings, different meanings, different problems, different solutions, different rules, different communities, different groups, different gods, different skills, different countries, different lands, different cultures, different rituals, different dressing style, different emotions, different pains, different kinds, different sins, different punishments, different treatments, different objectives, different subjects, different laws, different expressions, different hurdles, different paths, different approaches, different goals, different feelings, different colours, different shades, different species, different behaviours, different tears, different requirements, different tastes, different expectations, different races, different thoughts, different realities, different angers, different hungers, different abled, different skills, different talents, different stories, different access, different realities, different moments, different memories, different friends, different enemies, different journeys, different dreams, different days, different nights, different times, different different's.

Society is made up of multiple differences.

In a world of differences, everyone has their desires. Some people know how to fulfil and some adjust with what they have. But in our lives, some specific desires can't be adjusted when it is available and can be affordable in the world.

I have got so many different people as customers from then. Most of the people are married men and some are dons in the society.

I found one interesting thing about married people they are very afraid of coming here and having what they want. They don't want to spoil their name value in the society. So, they came silent and went silent. I always wonder why they behave like this. This a place that everyone knows in the society. People still visit here and don't want to tell anyone. Why is it like this?

I always wonder why people are not happy with their wives. Still why they are visiting here? If they are not happy with why they can't let go. Is this a kind of cheating? How they are attracted to us? Why society doesn't accept people coming here? Who created this in the first place if they don't accept it? Wonder questions.

Here I will explain to you one situation that happened in my life.

One day with mother went to a vegetable market. And of course, it was the first time for me to go to the market. My mother was searching for the quality of vegetables at a shop and I was looking around the market to observe how it is.

One uncle was coming with his family wife and daughter who was a little far away from us. Coming towards us. He didn't see me and reached the shop where we were buying.

He looked like a very formal and respectable man in society which was shown by his dressing. His wife is beautiful and has a wonderful daughter. They both were looking for quality vegetables.

After a few seconds, he turned around and looked at me.

That's it.

The expressions on his face were slowly changing. Within no time his face shows a tremendous fear and his eyes get bigger. I didn't understand why his face turned like that. He was worried like hell after seeing me. Maybe he thought he was living his last moments at that time. I was observing him very closely with anxiety because of his random behavior suddenly. He covered his wife and daughter. I was looking at him like I was going to wish him in that place in front of his wife and daughter. My anxiety and expressions towards him make him terrified. He started sweating and his legs were dancing out of fear. I didn't understand why he was behaving like that. But still, I'm observing his behavior which makes him more uncomfortable. He didn't speak a single word. In a few minutes, he was sweating like hell and worried very much. That I understood. But I don't know why.

My mother turned back and said, "Come, we will go to another shop".

We both left the shop and reached the new shop which was a little far away from the previous one.

After reaching, my mother started looking for different vegetables. And I turned around and started looking at him again.

He was watching us silently to know whether we were left or not. But when I turned back at him, he suddenly turned his head and talked to the shop person.

One thing I understood clearly was that he was terrified by seeing me and my behavior there in front of his family. Maybe he was expecting either of us to leave that place soon.

UNSOLD VIRGIN

After that incident, getting more customers like him, I started speaking to them about specific things to understand. Most people are never interested in sharing anything about them. Even sometimes they say false names to us. But few are there who can share their stories with us. But I never found one. I am looking for that one person who can share their stories and clear my doubts.

But one day I encountered one word which I never heard and that was the first time. Some random person came and asked our owner "Is there any Virgin here?".

My owner replied, "No".

I was struck by that word. What does it mean?

After he left, I asked my owner about the meaning of the word.

She harshly replied, "Go and do your work".

However, I was not able to control my anxiety.

I ran to my mom and asked her.

"Maa, what is the meaning of Virgin?" I asked.

"That is not for you, don't worry about that. Leave it", she said.

I understood that she was not going to tell me.

My brain was filled with more and more anxiety to know the meaning, but I found no one who was going to explain it to me clearly. My nerves got heated up.

I was shouting in my mind like "Is there anyone to explain this?"

I understood no one was at my place.

Days were passing. The customers I was getting were not even ready to talk for some time. So, no result for me.

But one day a person came who was a little younger than the regular ones.

He was not able to ask properly what he wanted. Our owner is a little arrogant and was not happy with his behavior. Started raising her voice on him. I understood that it was his first time.

With a fearful voice, he said that it was his first time and wanted to experience something like this with a new one. My owner understood his fear and started a quirky laugh at him.

She called my name Prashna and introduced me to him.

"She is the new one here", she said.

He stared at me and said, "Okay".

The owner told me to take him inside. I showed him the path to the room.

We both entered the room. I closed the doors. And started observing him from top to bottom. Looks like he is an educated person. His dressing style is different from the previous customers and he has combed hair. I took him onto the bed and sat facing each other. He moved a little back on the bed. He was not ready to sit closer. He was afraid of sitting next to me.

I asked his name. He said, "Satya".

"What do you do?", I asked.

"I have completed my studies and looking out for a job in the city nearby which was 109 KM away from this town", he said.

"Do you have a girlfriend?", I asked.

"No", he said.

UNSOLD VIRGIN

I wondered and asked why.

He was not ready to share that with me. I understood that.

"Do you know English", I asked.

"Yes", he said with a lower tone.

I just wanted to know the meaning of one word. Would you tell me that?

"If I know I will tell you that", he said.

I asked him "What is the meaning of Virgin?", with anxiety and excitement.

He observed my anxiety while I was asking that. Unfortunately, he thought that I was Virgin because my owner told me that I was the new one here.

"Are you a Virgin?", he asked with a little surprise and excitement.

I was like "Idiot, I asked you the meaning of that word and you are asking me back again".

I said, "Tell me the meaning first then I will tell you".

"That is the word where people use when a girl had sex never before in her lifetime", he said.

Out of curiosity, I asked, "Why only a girl?"

"I don't know but the society used to treat like that only", he said.

"Who is society?", I asked him.

"We, people living out there", he replied.

"Are we there in that we?", I asked him.

He was silent for a bit and said "Yeah, everyone included".

I smiled.

"I want to tell you one thing", I said.

"Yes", he said.

"As per the meaning you told I am not a virgin", I said.

A little facial expression on his face had changed but was brought back to normal in seconds. Maybe after seeing my excitement and the questions I asked him; he may think that I was a Virgin.

In my mind also I lost the anxiety after got to know the meaning of the word. Because I know that was lost way before in my life. But brings back my mood to normal because he was my customer and I should make him happy.

"Come, we'll start", I said.

Suddenly something struck my mind that he was doing this for the first time. Little bit excited.

"You are a virgin right", I asked him out of excitement even though it was confined to women in society.

"Yeah", he said with a shy smile.

We both started our thing. I felt that he was so nervous and afraid of doing it. And also, he never experienced a woman touch in such type of situation in his life. He tried but it was not happening. Maybe he just wants to experience it out of interest. No emotional thing was there in his thoughts as of that moment. I felt he was also just like another man who comes here regularly for their needs.

It's over. Nothing happened. He got upset because this was his first experience and it was a disaster. His expressions say everything about how much he was disappointed that day without saying a single word. Maybe there was a war going on in his mind at that moment. Because that's what introverts do.

He left with an upset mood.

I thought he would never come here again.

After he left my mind was flooded with a lot of questions. As usual, no one was there to answer them. But I continued thinking about them. My questions were sometimes irritating for me also but I couldn't be able to stop them from flowing through my brain.

I have recollected his answer. If anyone did the sex thing for the first time then we lost our virginity. Then here comes questions to me.

Was it only for a sex thing?

Or it can be applied to everything?

There are so many things in our lives that we do for the first time. Why does society never use that word in those things?

What happens if we use that in other things?

Has anyone tried ever before?

Who stops using that word in other things?

How it was created?

Who comes up first with that word?

What made him create a word like that which only caters to women?

Did people think it was made for only women?

How were women accepted this in society?

Or the people who created this was powerful?

How much powerful?

What is powerful?

How they were powerful?

Why do they use their power to create such a thing?

I always feel that one friend should be there to share all these kinds of things. Otherwise, our brains stop working out of the anxiety and pressure of not having the answers.

I'm back after those thought-provoking thoughts. Regular.

Meaningful meanings are Meaningless. Because they change.

REAL MEANING

Days were passing as usual. Customers are coming and going like a day and a night.

If you observe Hunger and Sleep are the only things which doesn't require our permission to come into our lives. Because we didn't even have a consciousness while experiencing them for the first time. After coming out of the safest darker place which was mother's womb we started to cry and then sleep. In a few days, the mother starts feeding the baby with her milk which also we never understood at that age. Later solid food was given to us after a few months. Then follows so many other things that we didn't do with consciousness. Those are fine because that comes with situations and time.

Also, we never know when our first period is going to come in life. Sleep-Hunger-Sex are the three most important elements and the only elements that come with birth. But Sleep-Hunger enters into our lives along with our birth. They don't require a certain time when our bodies need to get ready to enter into our lives.

Only for sex, our bodies need to get ready for the thing. I don't know who designed our bodies but exactly after certain years when our bodies are ready, it gives a signal called Periods. Maybe this is the only thing that we can do with consciousness out of the three elements in our life. Maybe it needs some maturity, preparedness, motive, energy to carry a baby, time to understand nature, what is it for, why is it for, and many other things.

If we go through our emotions, we never understand the first Sleep and Hunger experiences. But we have a greater chance to experience this element to the fullest with our hearts because with consciousness we are accepting of having sex. So that we can enjoy it to the fullest. But don't know how many are satisfied with their first time. You know mine, right?

Conscious Sex is a beautiful experience

There are certain first things that we can enjoy with consciousness. Like First Job, First Salary, First Sex, First moments with a person, etc.

But here the most important thing is whether you are feeling that high emotion with those first moments. We do so many first things because of society's rules but never do with our interest.

Let me give you an example.

The writer of this book has completed his graduation in Civil Engineering and doing a job. But he always wanted to become a Writer and Director for a Film. How can it be possible with a Graduation degree in Civil Engineering? No right? You know he never enjoyed his first Job moments because he was not interested. Due to some situations, he was doing his job. But one day he realizes because of a friend, why he shouldn't give it a try in Writing. Because he badly wants to write stories where he can enjoy the moment of writing them. Slowly he started writing and while doing it he really felt that happiness moments in his mind. That's where he found his real satisfaction. And the other thing was this was his first book. I'm glad that he chose my story to write as his first book which makes him happier. He found his highness here.

He's enjoying it.

First moments are always special but it doesn't mean that we enjoy our every first moment. Whenever we enjoy heartfully, then that is our real moment.

Let's come back to my story.

After a few days, Satya came back.

This time I thought he would choose another person. But he told my name to our owner.

I came out of the room and I was a little surprised after seeing him there.

We both entered the room and closed the door.

I was looking at him. He asked, "What happened?"

"Nothing, I thought you wouldn't come back again to me", I replied.

He was silent. We both sat on the bed and started talking.

"Tell me what made you come again here?", I asked.

He started answering, "Last time I was upset and not able to take it. I wanted to have a good experience but didn't happen. So, I want to try again".

"Why do you want this now?", I asked.

"I never had a girlfriend and don't know about so many things. Because of my introverted nature, I'm not good at contacting girls. And I am not able to control my feelings now. I have researched about how to get relief from those strong feelings. I found this is the one way", he replied.

"Then why did you come to me again, you can choose another one right?", I asked.

"Just now I told you, I am not good at approaching. Already we both met last time, so, I choose to come back to you again", he answered.

I feel he is something different than the others who regularly came here. He wanted to have an experience but I also thought he was immature. Anyway, this is my job of giving pleasure to people who came to us.

"Are you okay today?", I asked.

"Yeah, yeah I'm okay", he said.

"Okay then, we can start", I told him.

We both were doing and after some time he caught up very fast. Again, he was very upset about not having a proper one. Maybe if I wouldn't have been there, he may have started crying there. I was able to see his expressions. He was controlling his frustration, and anger, and not able to take this defeat.

He left silently again.

After he left, I started thinking again about him. He was so disturbed in his life. He feels that no one is attracted to him and not ready to spend time with him because of his introverted nature. But he was unable to come out of that. I felt that people around him were enjoying their lives with their girlfriends by going to parties, and movies, traveling together, been there for their friends. Maybe he has no friends who can understand him properly. Due to these reasons, he was alone and crying lonely.

I don't understand why people around him behave like that. Why they don't care about him when he was with them? What kind of pressures he was facing? Or Am I wrong? His friends were ready to mingle with him but he was not. What's going on with this person?

By seeing these kinds of people, I always wonder how this society is made up.

These are never-ending questions in my brain.

Out of surprise, Satya came once again. We both entered the room and closed the doors.

This time he was looking a little weird. He was filled with frustration and anger, a little confidence to prove himself.

We have started our work. But the result was the same on that day too.

He was busted out that day. Started crying slowly. Holding his grip very tight with anger and helplessness. He started acting weird which made me afraid that day. I felt that he was going to do something to me. He was acting like that. Later he calmed down and sat on the bed.

In this gap, I felt that I was wrong about society after seeing his behavior. Maybe he was not allowing anyone into his life. He makes him alone by himself. And he has a lot of pain in him but he doesn't want to share his pain with anyone. Because of unbearable pain within him, he shows anger and irritation when people approach him. I understood this from his behavior because sometimes I also feel the same in my life. But I don't know exactly what he was going through in his life.

Hard times. No friends. Most Painful thing ever.

After a few minutes, he became normal and sat silent. He wiped his tears.

"What happened to you?", I asked him.

He started telling his story after a huge internal fight within him.

"You know when I was a child, I had a friend's gang in our colony and we used to live together. In those days we didn't know what we were doing but enjoyed ourselves a lot. After a few years, I don't know exactly what happened, my friends started to tease me about everything. Whatever I say, they turned it into a joke. I thought I was doing something wrong but later realized that teasing me because of their new friendships at school. I didn't understand what was happening. Every day I used to cry at home. I couldn't say this to my parents. The fact was I didn't know how to tell them because they were friends. Gradually I became silent because of that. From then I never spoke to anyone even at school unless I felt comfortable with and trusted them. Likewise, I'm afraid of talking to girls. Because of those fears I never approached them by thinking What if they don't like me and laugh at me? I never even dare to look at them. Additionally, there are a lot of things happening in my which haunt me every day. Loneliness used to take care of me in those hard times. We both became best friends. We can't live without each other. That became my life partner also. You know growing up with loneliness was very dangerous. It never allows us to become stronger, to communicate with people, to think better, to be positive, to increase contacts, and sometimes you also forget how to talk to people. This brings you real loneliness. Never allows you to grow in society. People find it very difficult to understand you when you are not ready to mingle with them. We never get a chance to blame them for not understanding us. But I always feel at least one person should be there who can understand us without saying any words. I never found one. Do you know Karna in Indian mythology called Mahabharata? I had a strong feeling of this every day. After Arjuna chopped the head of Karna, the omnipresent person called Krishna, why didn't he go near the head of Karna and hold his life for a minute and ask, "Do you have any last wish Karna?". To this as a reply, Karna could have replied, "Vasudeva (Krishna), you know everything, I don't have any wishes regarding hell or heaven but I have one wish to ask you, that is, more than anyone you know about my life story in all lives, but in this life, I had gone through so many hurdles and convicted as a liar, had so many curses for which I was not aware. In my entire life, I never had a person with whom I could share my pain and lay my head on their shoulder. I wanted to share my pain with you through my own words for one last time. I will never be able to find a person who can understand my pain more than you. Even though you know everything please let me express the pain in my own words. And I don't have hands now to request you to write my story with your own hands through my words. This is my last wish Vasudeva". Why didn't Krishna accept his last wish and write the pain of Karna as a story in Karna's words with his own hands? After that, he should have allowed his head to die. If this happened that day, maybe we all know the real pain of a Karna in his words, and also people understand that even god listened to the pain of a human. After this, people could have asked their friends about their pain and listened to understand them in today's world as the mighty god Krishna listened to Karna even if he knew everything. If no one was there for you like that, then this is the most painful thing you have ever faced in your life", he said.

I started crying after listening to this. Because I also had no one to share. Everyone knows everything about us but never understands. That day I understood he had a lot of pain in him.

"Don't worry", I said. All I can say is that.

He gave a small smile and said, "I'm used to it, you don't worry about me".

He got up and dressed himself and left the room.

I can feel his pain. Not to the fullest but we are traveling on the same path in different lives.

You know everything. But let them Speak.

After a few days, a festival came which is very auspicious to the people. Our streets were empty. Finally, we got a full time to talk to our colleagues and share some feelings.

But unexpectedly a customer came for one of our colleagues and I was surprised because he visited on the day of the festival. He spent three hours with her on the festival day. I had already seen him before coming regularly for her. I was surprised How could a person come regularly for a person in our business line? I wanted to know the secret behind this.

I was busy with my work. After a few minutes, Satya came. I was out of my mind after seeing that day. I don't know what was going on with him, but he was deeply disturbed because of his failures earlier.

"What happened to your mind? Why today?", I asked him very angrily.

"Nothing, I'm very upset and not able to control my mind. Until I'm successful in that I can't be normal again. This is my mindset. Even I'm not able to focus on other things", he replied.

Firstly, I got angry, and later understood his mindset and situation which was happening with him. Slowly I started laughing at him.

I told him to wait for ten minutes as I was doing some work at that time. He sits on the chair which was at our hall.

After ten minutes, I called him and both went inside the room. I was laughing at him because of his behavior. Because I have never seen such a person in my life. He was a little different person than I face every day. Every other person comes for pleasure but this man was coming to get his first experience.

On that day he was in a different temperament and looked like he was filled with confidence to achieve something. We have started doing it. From the start itself, he was different that day. His approach was different that day. Doing new things, taking his own time, handling with care, and there is an ease of doing it. I felt the difference. Finally, we have reached the moment where we could reach heaven. It's done.

He lay beside me on the bed taking a deep breath and releasing it slowly. After a minute, he asked me, "How was it today?".

I don't know but that day I felt something that I didn't expect from him. He was fully prepared and wanted to have sex with me and be successful. And he did it.

"You did it nicely today", I replied.

"Don't lie. Please tell me the truth", he asked with enthusiasm.

I turned towards him on the bed and looked at him.

"Today you have done it better than so many people who come here", I told him.

At that moment, I was observing his facial expressions. His face was filled with super satisfaction like he achieved the greatest toughest thing in the world. He was super happy at that moment. Out of that happiness, he dragged me back, held my head tightly, and gave me a tight kiss on my cheek for around ten seconds.

That's it.

I had never felt that feeling in my life. When he held my head tightly and kissed me on the cheek, I felt a different vibe in my body. Not even my mother did that before. Even though I had sex with many people but never felt that warm feeling. There was a little shock and excitement inside my mind forcing my body to feel the kiss to its fullest level.

This was the feeling he wanted and he got that day with me. There was a little pride on his face. I liked that.

If you plan a miracle, it will be a disaster.

If you are ready for a disaster, it will be a miracle.

After coming out of that high moment, he left from there.

I also got down from the bed and started doing my work.

I am looking for my colleague whether she came out or not. After some time, they both came out of the room.

He left.

She was busy with her work for a while. In the evening after completing all our work we both sit together for a chit-chat.

I asked her, "I was observing for a while, why he is coming to you only, I had never seen him look for another woman here. What's the secret?"

"Oh, he is my regular customer who has been coming for the last three years. In these years we created some bond that's why he never looked for another woman here. And also, he was a married person", she said.

"How did that bond develop between you if he was married?", I questioned her.

She started saying, "Initially he came three years ago, you know he was very arrogant and didn't even speak to me properly. He always looks out for what he came here and leaves. I felt he was a little weird person. I decided not to take such customers again but there is no choice for us here. He used to come again and again and chose me. I didn't understand why he was choosing me every time. After a few times, he opened up about himself, and from then he started speaking properly to me. He has two kids who are going to school. His wife was not doing a job and took care of his family at home. He already has financial issues and top of that his child's educational fees. This a society that was upgraded in past years and education is a must for every child to survive in the future. No one cares whether you are stable in your financials or not but you should do everything that others who are financially stable are doing. Society creates that kind of culture. And in those pressure times, not everyone gets a wife who understands and supports them at low moments. Or maybe she has some different thoughts in her mind for her children's future. After a time, they both thought that they were not understanding each other which created disturbance and depression in them. He has an option of coming here. One day he revealed everything to me. From then he was normal and created some bond between us. We both had a good time.

One day he came very peaceful and maybe his tensions were cleared at that moment. He said, "I'm happy today, we will do it in my way".

I thought he was happier today and I accepted. And also, we don't have a choice, right? To that day also I'm looking at him as a customer who is coming for his benefits.

We both went inside the room.

We sit on the bed and face each other.

He holds my hand and gently touches it. He asked, "Can I kiss you?"

I was surprised by that question.

After having sex so many times, he was asking my permission to kiss me. I felt a little excited but also worried at the same time.

I said yes.

He asked me to close my eyes. Another shock of the day. With a little excitement, I closed my eyes. And I was expecting that he was going to kiss me on my lips. But a third shock happened that day which was a bigger one.

He kissed me on my neck by holding my hand gently. And told me to open my eyes.

"How do you feel?", he asked me romantically.

"Nothing feels different", I replied.

That was the first shock to him. His expression made me laugh that day.

He asked, "What? You felt nothing?".

"Yes", I said.

He said, "Close your eyes again".

I did.

This he took a little more care and kissed my neck again on another spot.

"How is it now?", he asked.

"Same", I replied.

He was shocked by my answers and stared at me for some time.

"Don't lie, tell me the truth", he asked a little seriously.

"If I felt something, why should I lie about it", I replied.

He was worried.

This time he touched my waist and gently applied pressure with his fingers.

I understood one thing he got upset for not getting what he expected from me.

To his satisfaction, this time I made a moaning sound when he touched my waist gently by closing my eyes. I felt that he slowly took back his by gently dragging his fingers on my waist. I am continuing the sounds.

A few seconds later I felt nothing from his hand and opened my eyes.

He was staring at me with a serious face.

"What are you doing?", he asked.

After that question, I was not able to control my laugh. Laughed out loud.

But he was looking at me seriously.

"Why are you laughing? What made you laugh like that?", he asked.

"What are you doing today? Are you drunk? You are doing different things which doesn't make any sense. Why should I feel different when you kiss me on my neck?", I said.

"What are you talking? Wait, have you ever experienced someone kissing your neck and touching your waist sensibly?", he asked.

"Why do people do those things here and that too to us?", I replied.

"Also, I've been working here for six years and no one ever did that to me. I thought this was the process for sex that we are used to. And no one ever cares about feelings here. Only needs", I added.

Needs have no feelings but Wants have.

He sat silent for a moment. Head down. Maybe he was thinking about our situation here.

"You have never felt these feelings?", He asked again.

"No, never till now, even with you also before", I replied.

By that reply, he got hurt for his previous actions and understood what people were doing to us here. He felt very sad about that.

"I am sorry for what I have done previously", he said.

That was a big blow for me that day. I Should remember that day in my lifetime because, for the first in my life, someone was saying sorry here in this place to us. I was surprised a lot.

"Will you allow me to teach you something", he asked me.

I thought today something I was going to learn new things from him and I was excited about that.

"Yes", I said.

That day he was holding my hand gently and started slowly kissing on my neck. Then he slowly moves to my cheeks. Along with that, his fingers are playing music on my navel softly. He touches my entire body with his fingers and slowly makes movements like kids walking their first steps who don't know about their next steps where to put. He skilfully played with my body that day. Did that for a while.

We both were done after some time. He was eagerly waiting for my response after that.

"How was it?", he asked me.

"You know I didn't feel anything today because of my past handling by people", I said. His face was a little upset.

And also added, "But today I found a person who can handle the woman's body differently, that I liked it. This was the first time I had experienced a smooth and gentle touch after many huge ugly battles with different people. Allow me some time to get prepared. My body needs some time to get back those feelings".

He nods his head. We will try our next time. He said and left.

Right from then, I was thinking about my past and what have I done to my body. Why I am not able to react to those actions?

Has my body forgotten about those feelings or they are not manufactured in my body?

I had asked so many people about how we got them back. But no answer from anyone here because they are all like me only. I was thinking and breaking my brain to know about how we get them back like searching for a wall in the air.

I was not able to eat and sleep properly. It was irritating to me and haunting me.

UNSOLD VIRGIN

Why didn't I meet this person before?

Why now?

Why did he tell me about those feelings?

Why I'm not able to control my mind?

Ahhhhh! It was irritating.

I was ready to take customers also. Our owner was shouting at me every day because of my behavior. But nothing could stop me from thinking.

One day an old customer who was in his age of seventies came here. Everyone was shocked. And no one was ready to take him as a customer. Our owner got irritated and called me by shouting. When I reached there after seeing him, I was also shocked and understood something that the owner was selecting me for him. I was a bit worried and hesitated to not go. But our owner shouted at me to take him as a customer.

Everyone was laughing that day and I felt very embarrassed in front of everyone.

I held his hand and took him into the room.

He was shaking while walking. I was worried about his health condition.

"Why did you come here?", I asked him.

I helped him to sit on the bed. He started answering my question very slowly.

"My wife passed away ten years back due to health issues, since then I have been feeling very lonely and my kids are staying away from me. Being alone was very dangerous and thoughts would kill us. So, I just wanted to get the woman touch feeling once for the last time in my life. That's why I came here", he replied.

I have no words to say about that except I feel for his loneliness.

Some sparks have been sparked in my brain. How he could get the feelings now after ten years of no such touch from a woman? I wondered about this question because the same situation was happening in my life.

I was not able to control myself for asking that question to him.

"Can I ask you a question?", I asked.

He nods his head slowly.

"How can you feel with me the same way you used to feel once upon a time? Because you haven't touched any woman in the last ten years, how is that possible now?", I asked him.

I was eager to know the answer.

He gave me an excellent answer to that question. I wonder if I could ever give a thought like that. Maybe that is called the experience.

"See, if you want to taste the best of something that you like very much, you should prepare your body and hunger for that", he replied.

I thought WoW! But how to prepare for that?

"How is that possible if we are doing the same thing regularly for years?", I asked him.

"Take a break", he replied.

"Why are you asking these questions?", he asked me.

"I want to experience the same with a person", I replied.

He was silent for a minute. Maybe he was thinking about what to do now because I told him that I was waiting to feel those moments in my life.

He understood my intentions and decided something.

"I am leaving, you get to prepare yourself for those moments. I can understand that you have never experienced those feelings. I had many moments with my partner. Don't worry, I will be okay", he said.

He left and didn't complain to our owner. Good old person.

I have started thinking about how to get prepared. For that, I should stop taking customers for a while. But our owner never allows that at any cost. I was thinking of an idea. At that time one person here got ill and took her to hospital. The owner was not sending customers to her because of illness. I liked that idea and applied it.

I succeeded but not for a long time. It was about eight days since I took the customer. The owner was upset about me and getting irritated because of my actions. She used to shout at me every day.

And that was the time he didn't come for a long time. Another fear starts in my mind. Because I was not taking customers and having sex with any other person for those moments but the person I wanted was not coming. I waited for a few more days, but our owner's pressure increased and I was not able to hold it further. I thought maybe he lost interest in me because of that day and didn't want to meet me again. I was almost upset and didn't know what to do nothing but waiting for him.

I thought he would never come back.

That was the last day for me as an exception from our owner. She was about to kick me out of this place if I didn't take customers the next day. I have decided that maybe we will never be able to enjoy that kind of moment in our lives. I was upset.

On next day I lost hope and prepared myself to come back and do my job as usual but when I came out of the room he was standing in the hall and looking for me. At that moment I couldn't explain my happiness and was not able to hold my feelings. Very much excited.

It makes me feel like my life has come back to give me those moments at least once. It was the happiest day of my entire life.

He was talking to our owner and looking out for me. After a while, our owner called me and asked to take him. I said 'Okay'.

We both entered the room. Closed the doors.

I was not in control and wanted to hug him very tightly but couldn't do that because of limits. My brain was creating multiple feelings and fighting with each other inside me. I'm helpless.

My eyes were about to roll out tears of joy and enthusiasm after seeing him but didn't flow out to my cheeks. He was observing my face and reading my emotions. He was staring at me for a minute with awkward silence in the room.

On that day, I felt a soothing sound of waves hitting me continuously from inside in the silent place. I was like having feelings and emotions as water in the ocean that never be able to hold still even for a second and releasing that pressure in the form of waves at the edges. But I'm in a position where I cannot allow that feeling wave to come out of my eyes and trying to hold still. By passing time they are turning into a Tsunami which I cannot be able to hold further. I need some help to hold them back inside me for a while and slowly release them while experiencing to enjoying the moment. There he comes, near me, and whispers in my ears, "Close your eyes", in a deep voice that made my feelings turn into a tsunami.

"Are you ready for this moment today?", he whispered in my ears with a deep romantic voice which made my body start vibrating. I have never felt that before which was more exciting and increased my anxiety at the moment.

He was removing my saree without touching the body with his hands. Walking around me while unboxing me from my clothes very silently. That sense of silence in the room generates more feelings inside me. That calmness with ready to burst out feeling, never experienced in my life.

Stands exactly in front of me at an inch's distance. He said, "Don't open your till I say".

He was creating an atmosphere surrounded by romance which can pass feelings through air and sounds between us. I can feel his aura and a beautiful smell from him. Everything was added as an ingredient for pressurizing my feelings and increase enthusiasm to experience it more. While whispering in my ears he slowly started gently touching my hands and smoothly moving up and down in a rhythm. That sensible and unexpected touch makes me take a deep breath which wakes up my nerves to experience it deeper. Smoothly he was cycling his fingers to my shoulders, applied gentle pressure on my shoulder, and came a little forward and asked, "Is this working?".

I was not even in that position to say YES because my body was shivering with emotions and feelings. I nodded my head with closed eyes in a way that meant YES and bit my lips.

Maybe he understood the feelings I was going through. He didn't say a word after that. He continued his work. He came behind me and slowly kept his hands on my shoulder. Started kissing on my shoulder, moving towards my neck by kissing inch by inch from shoulder. Every kiss makes me feel high till it reaches my neck. When he kissed on neck, my body gave a small jerk kind of feeling because of that sensible kiss.

Started kissing every inch of my body. Feelings were passing through the nerves at unimaginable speed. He pushes onto the bed. Played with his fingers on my navel while it was dancing. He sits on me. Removed his shirt. Hold my hands tightly above my head and play with my jacket hooks. Those sensible touches are awesome and I missed those in my life. I have allowed very few to kiss on my lips. He was one of them. That day I was waiting from inside for the kiss on my lips but he was playing with my body. Everything was a surprise for me at that moment. Playing with my navel removing the hooks of my jacket, kissing my neck, and all of sudden, kissing me on my lips with pressure makes my soul partly leave my body. It started from there. He leaves my hands and sets me free. I was not able to control myself and into the game deeply. We both were having fun like never experienced but it was a thrill to me.

That day I felt that I was made for him.

I had sensed every feeling of touch which made my body awaken from the dead ash. It was a wonderful moment ever in my life.

Maybe if he had not come to me, I would never have had such an experience till I die. From then there was a bond created between us which made us a little more comfortable while having those beautiful moments.

That was the first time I enjoyed having sex till that point in my life. No one ever asked me about my feelings or asked me whether I was ready to do it or not. Maybe he came into my life to teach me about the feelings and emotions that every person should feel at least once in a lifetime".

This was the story behind their bonding. I observed one thing while she was telling her story, she was happy while telling her bond with him. Maybe that kind of person is needed in everyone's life to awaken us out of something where we all were buried.

I felt that day when she enjoyed wholeheartedly with her favorite person, that day she lost her virginity ever in her life.

Later I went back to my story and recollected the feelings I got when Satya kissed me on my cheek with some happy excitement that day. He planted a seed in me that day. Maybe the feelings were still awakened in my body and that was a signal to me.

Or maybe I thought I was overthinking of scene that happened between me and Sathya. I don't know but I was not able to conclude.

I moved on and started my work after the festival. As usual, our business line got normal when the festival ended. Customers were coming regularly. I was taking a few of them. While I was having sex with them, I couldn't feel the same as with Sathya. I don't know why but every customer was like coming doing and going. Just like that. I felt that no one was ready to build a bond with me like Sathya did. And also, sometimes I felt that I was thinking too much and it would be alright in a few days. But no such thing has happened. Again, in dilemma.

As she did, I took a break from the work and started exploring myself. Thinking about the senses, feelings, and emotions that she went through. Maybe I took this decision very early than her because it was too late for her. But for me, feelings were aggressive and hitting the shores continuously.

After a few days, I realized that I couldn't hold myself back, maybe Sathya was the person in my life who could do the same thing which happened to my colleague. I came to this conclusion because I'm not finding those moments with any other person maybe he was the one.

And ironically, Sathya was not visiting for two weeks. I don't know what happened to him. I was worried. I thought he would come maybe next week. But no. Didn't come. Then I remembered Satya saying that he was going to his city and didn't know when he would come back.

A small fear started with me because after having those feelings and imaginations with him,

What if he didn't show off?

What should I do?

Where should I go?

Whom can I approach to know about him?

Where does he live?

How can I reach him?

Did anything happen to him?

Why he was not coming?

Did he go somewhere out of town?

If so, which place?

So many questions chasing me and letting me down from the hope. Don't know what to do next. I was done with my mother and owner. They both were kind of torturing me for not taking the customers for almost three weeks then. I couldn't be able to hold them for more time. I was frustrated because of their behavior and decided to leave that place and start searching for Sathya. Didn't know whether he would come or not. For the first time, I made a brave decision to leave my home place for Sathya.

Yes, I have decided on my plan. I left the home.

Due to an earthquake, the droplet of water in the pond starts flowing through the breakage of the ground and joins in the continuously flowing river with a certain speed which eventually joins in the ocean of dirt.

Feelings can lead to any kind of extent

KNOWING SOCIETY

Stepping out for the first time by expecting a greater good.

I once remember he was from the city which was a little far away from our village. Around 109 KM from my hometown. I had some money which I saved from my work and a new saree I bought for myself and took the bus to the city.

It was all new to me because I had never crossed the border of our area and of course, it was not necessary. I was wondering about everything that comes our way to the city. Buses were new to me, there were autos, horse-rickshaws, bikes, cars, different kinds of buildings, people, and many more. Somewhere in my mind, I was deeply afraid of leaving home without knowing anything about him and the city. I don't even know how people are in the city, whether they are helpful or not. So many things were running in my mind. Sat silently on the bus till the city arrived.

City arrived. The conductor was calling everyone to get down as that was the last stop for the bus.

My heart skipped a heartbeat for a moment when he said that. I was worried to get down but I have no option. Slowly got down from the bus. I was afraid to enter the bus station because it was very big and fully crowded. The conductor who was in his near sixties was observing me and asked me,

"New to the city?".

I said, "Yes".

"Do you know anyone here?", he asked.

"No", I said.

"Then why did you come here?", he asked.

"I was looking for someone who used to come to our house?", I replied.

"Do you have his address?", he asked.

"No", I said.

"Without having any address how can you find him in this big city", he asked.

I was silent for a minute. Someone called him. While leaving he said, "Take a look, if you didn't find his address come here and take the same bus to your home back".

He was the first person who talked to me in that city. He was a nice person. The first person I met was nice so I thought everyone in the city would be nice.

I stepped into the city. Oh my god, everything was a miracle to me here. Big shops, buildings, bridges, autos, and cars are bigger than those I saw on my way to the city. Now the important thing to me was searching for Satya in this big city. I don't know how but I need to find him as early as possible.

I sat at some place and ate some food which was available on the roadside. Thinking about how to search for him and where I can start in this very big city. I started asking some questions to the food place owner.

"Brother, where can I find students who completed their education and are looking for a job?", I asked him.

He mentioned three places where a large number of students live and look for jobs in that city which were also a little far from the place I was.

After eating I started. On my way to those places, I was observing everything in the city. Maybe it was around 9'O clock in the morning that day, some shops were open and the majority were closed. I don't know the time when the other shops will get opened. But they were very big. In our place, one shop would cover the entire vegetable market. That big.

I have reached one of the places where students were found. It was almost around 11:30 AM. There was a huge gathering of students who were roaming the streets with their friends and partners by holding their hands each other. I was afraid after seeing the students. I lost hope for a second whether I could be able to find him or not. Still brought some boost along with hope. Moving forward. Searching every gang and faces of students. Some were watching at me like an alien was roaming on the roads.

I couldn't be able to find Sathya in that place. I needed to go to the next place but it was a little far away from that place. I asked for the area name from someone in the student's gang and took the shared auto to reach that place. While traveling in the auto, some girls got into the auto and one of them was talking on the phone. After listening to her conversation, I understood that she was talking to her boyfriend. After a minute she got another call and she said to the person that she was talking to her brother.

I was literally shocked. I felt what was happening here. And surprised. But I sat silent and observed the city.

I have reached the place. I get down and look out for the way. At a distance of vision, a huge building was there with all the banners attached to the building. Later I got to know that was the coaching area for students. Sat there for a while looking at all the students coming and going. It was very difficult to observe every person out there but still, I was doing that.

I was there till the afternoon and had my lunch there at the roadside shop. Didn't find him. I was thinking of going to the next place. I got the auto again and sat in the auto.

Reached third place but it was near to the previous one. But I didn't know that. We could reach the third place by walking also.

It was filled with Coffee shops, restaurants, Tea shops, and bakeries. Many couples were there sitting and enjoying their time with their loved ones. I went to one shop that was on the corner and had a sitting place outside from where we could see the roadside.

I sat there and observed the people. My eyes were filled with hope for Sathya.

You know, whenever we are looking for something that can't be found even that was there in front of us or nearby place. I don't know how this logic works. I don't know what to do in that city if I don't find Sathya.

I was afraid of where could I stay in that city. I thought I would ask someone about the stay at a nearby place. I went to one of the roadside food makers, and asked him, "Was there any facility to stay for this night?".

He replied, "There was a lodge nearby to that place which was about half a kilometer from there.

I was tired from the day and started to reach the lodge to stay.

I reached the lodge. When I was entering the lodge a couple came outside. The man laid his hands on her shoulder. I thought that was a good place to stay as couples are also visiting. I entered and took the room for a day. Entry done and entered the room. The rooms were okay but not that good.

UNSOLD VIRGIN

Sat on the bed. Hold my head due to a headache caused by roaming in the city throughout the day. The sounds, horns, and noise of people, all were new to me, and couldn't be able to take them.

Lay on the bed. Thinking deeply.

Whether the thing I did was correct or wrong?

What my mother was doing there?

How my owner was reacting to this?

What was she going to do to my mother?

If I go back, will they accept me or not to stay with them?

What will Sathya do if I find him?

Whether he will accept my proposal or not?

How does he react after seeing me here?

I was getting angry at myself because of all these questions to be asked before I left the house. With all these questions in my mind, I lost my hunger for the night. I slept.

The next day woke up and repeated the same thing that I had done the before day. But the result was the same. I was about to break down myself and couldn't control my cry. Busted out for not finding him and fear of not finding him.

On the third day, I repeated the same. Same result. My money was running out and getting very difficult to stay there. But one thing I came across while coming to my room.

While I was walking on the road to my room, to reach my room I should cross a street where all the families were living. One woman was beating a man like hell. I was watching such kind of scene for the first time and I stood there to know the issue. That woman was shouting, "What have I done to you? Why did you do this to me? I was taking care of you and your children well but you still went for another woman. While shouting she slapped him on the cheek. She holds his shirt collar and drags him. Crying loudly in the street. Everyone was watching. Children don't know why their mother was beating their father. She was yelling at him. Asking for reasons and her mistakes. Poor man he was standing silent and controlling her but she didn't let him to. He has a terrified face and is afraid of his wife. Looks like feeling guilty in front of his children.

That day I understood why the uncle in the market when I went with my mother was afraid out of his life when he saw me there. I realized that if I greeted him then the same situation would happen to him also. That too in front of his daughter who was my age. That was disgusting to them. No one could ever be able to take that embarrassment in front of their kids.

But why they are doing this? I don't have the answer to that.

I reached my room as usual disappointed for that day. Lay on the bed and thought about the next day. Will it be better than today? Can I find him?

In addition to that, I never thought about how people see us in society. Because I had never faced such a situation. Whether they were ready to talk to us in front of their family or friends on the roads and accept us as we are. I haven't even thought that one day I would face such kind of situation in my life.

The next day, maybe this will be my before last day in the city searching for Sathya because the money I got is nearly spent. There was no other option for me other than to leave the city if I didn't find him.

In that strong disbelief, I started my day searching for Sathya. That was a sunny day. My energy was draining and unable to walk properly. In addition to that a hopeless thought. With a lot of tiredness, I went to the small shop where they can sell cigarettes match-boxes, and snack items, along with water bottles. I bought the water bottle. I sat on the bench under the tree in front of a coffee shop. I drank some water and relaxed after the energy booster went in.

Out of nowhere, a thin person was walking on the street who exactly looked like Sathya. I was unable to recognize him in that position of mine. I took some time to clear my blur but till then that person went into the coffee shop. Later I thought he was not the person I was looking for. But for a moment my heart beat faster than usual after I had assumed resemblances of Sathya in that person.

After some time, that person came out walking with his friends. Now I was clear in seeing people. My heart was excited and started to run faster after seeing that person. Yes, He was Sathya. I couldn't explain my happiness in words at that moment. He was the only reason for me to leave home for the first time, enter such a big city in which I didn't know anything in the city, stay at dangerous hotels, strangers watching me on the roads, and lots of fear in my mind, hopeless soul while roaming on the roads searching for him, sleepless nights, and more.

I got all the energy and ran to Sathya and stood in front of him. I was waiting for his reaction when he saw me because there was a long gap between us after he visited our home. I thought he felt very happy and going to hug me after seeing me.

But things went differently which made me cry like hell.

He looks with stunned reaction after seeing me there in the city standing in front of him. His face turned into a shocked expression and later to a little nervous. Maybe he never expected me here in the city or come for him like this. His friends were watching me when I was looking at him. They again turned to him and watched in a surprise reaction.

They asked him, "Do you know her?".

He was not in a position to answer that question. His face started to get nervous and sweat was coming down his face. I thought he was afraid of introducing me to them.

But that's not the fact.

After a few seconds, he replied, "I don't know who she is?"

I was shocked and looked at him in silence. He was uncomfortable when I was there. Not even talking properly and his voice was shaking. Maybe he felt embarrassed in front of his friends when he saw me there. After listening to the harsh answer, I was able to connect all the things that happened to me in my life.

Now I understood why the uncle was silent when his wife beat him a day ago. Maybe Sathya only came to experience the feeling of sex. There was no relation between us other than Customer and Client. It hurts me a lot. Because I never thought that he saw me as a stranger and did not even talk to me. Maybe he felt ashamed to introduce me to his friends and explain what thing happened between us.

People are scared outside.

I didn't know what to say there when he said he didn't know me in front of his friends. I had never experienced such a situation and didn't know what to do at that moment.

Could I say "he was lying, we both know each other, and we had sex multiple times".

What happens next if I say that to them?

How do they react?

How do they see their friend?

What they will think about him?

Did they feel bad for him?

Did he tell his friends ever that he had sex with someone?

Do people share such things with friends?

What he will do after I say that?

Could he accept or not?

What he is thinking now?

Can he able to control his emotions like anger?

Is he going to slap me?

Awwwwww…..

Everything was running in my mind and I was silent. After he said that I understood he was rejecting me there and directly conveyed not to talk to him in front of his friends.

Politely said to me, "Please go away from here, don't come to me again".

I left from there.

They left.

I came and sat on the bench under the tree. My brain starts realizing everything. I can't control myself from crying. I didn't have faced such emotion in my life to deal with. Sathya was also one of the people in the society. I believed that he was nice to me at home and would treat me as his friend at least. But nothing happened except seeing him at least in that big city.

I had decided to go back to my home. Reached the hotel for my things. I entered the room and packed my things.

Unexpectedly, I heard people shouting and running in the corridors. I came out of the room with my bag, and all of a sudden, a lady police came and held my hand very tightly. I was shocked and terrified. They were even not allowing me to talk and not at all ready to listen to me. I was trying to explain to them that I came here to meet a person but they pushed me into their jeep and then took me to the police station.

There are other women and girls with me in the station. They were silent and did not say a single word. I didn't understand why they were silent in the police station. Later one constable was explaining the situation to the senior police and why they brought all of us to the station. I was worried after listening to that. Because I was not here for that purpose. Even though back at our house we did the same no police ever came and took us to the police station. I thought it was okay in the society. I didn't know that this was illegal in the city. Sometimes police people also came to us but here it was different. I didn't understand any of this and started crying.

My cry was filled with fear, aggression, and most importantly feelings of regret for leaving my home for this kind of society.

The senior police officer came to us and looked very seriously. He pointed out to me and asked who are you? We have never seen you before at that place. I didn't say a single word out of fear. A lady constable came to me and gave me a tight slap on my face. That's it. With that fear and pain, I was out of consciousness.

After a while, I came into consciousness. And I was sleeping on the bench in the police station. Then a lady police came to me, gave me some water and asked for my details. I told them all the details. They called my owner and talked about me.

By the next morning, our owner came to the police station. She was very angry at me. I was looking for my mother but she didn't come. Police handed over me to the owner. After that owner gave me a tight slap again but I didn't lose consciousness because of my previous experience.

Reality is really hard

BACK TO HOME

We have started back to our home. By that evening we reached our destination. My mother was waiting for me there. One thing I noticed that day that blew me out. My mother was crying for me sitting on the veranda. I never assumed that she would ever cry for me in my lifetime but that day broke my useless thoughts.

We entered our home.

She saw me and stood up while wiping her tears with her hands. She ran to me and started beating me wherever she wanted. And she continued crying even when she was beating me. That day I didn't understand why my mother reacted that much. Because I have never seen her in that mood crying for me or showing that much anger on me. Everything was confusing that day. She was not stopping beating me. In between owner involved and stopped her.

Finally, she stopped and hugged me very tightly. I hugged her back. That was a new feeling to me.

"Am I hugging my mother? Is this real today?"

Yes, it was real that day. But I don't know why at that moment.

Everything was settled down. I went inside the room. Took my time to calm down.

At night, I came out of the room and sat on the veranda. My mother came and still, she was angry with me. I don't when she would calm down. She came to me and slaps me again. I was shocked. Why she didn't calm down till now?

Then she started shouting at me.

"What do you think of yourself? Do you think you have grown enough to survive alone? Do you even know what the outside world is? How do they behave? How do they live? How do they talk? How do they judge? Have you ever thought that you could take care of yourself? Do you know what kind of people are out there?" all she asked while crying and beating me.

I was looking at her innocently with no answer. I don't what she was going to do next.

"Do you think I'm a fool and staying here silently? Do you think we don't know how to escape from here and live in the outside world? Or do you think we are fools and don't know how to live?", she added.

After these questions, I realized that she has gone through a lot in her life. I had started crying and watching the pain in her eyes. I had never seen her with these many emotions at a single time. But one thing I really understood was that she worried a lot for me when I left the home.

She calmed down and sat beside me. After a while, she stopped crying.

"You will never understand this world at your age. Everything was surprising and exciting to you but to the core, it is entirely different. Everyone is good to you when they want something from you. That too for women, they are like helping hands but not everyone. Maybe a few help you unintentionally. They didn't expect anything in return from you but to find them in the current world is difficult. And the society gets to know that you are a sex worker then the entire world is different to you. You need to face as many as insults possible until you die. But sometimes it feels like death is better than insults. Different people have different mentalities and perspectives. Everyone in society is good and intelligent until they join a group that eventually becomes a society where few people make decisions and tell others to follow. Society never gives you time to understand how it runs because once you understand then you are a stranger to that society. You are not a part of it. They will never treat you well, respect you, and accept you as one of them. The woman is only a sex toy in a society where some are at a place like us and others are at their place but the thought process is common. Outside the ocean is filled with each other's dumps. It is dirty everywhere except in a few places. This is why I returned here with loads of pain done by society. Here we are not making any mistakes. We are doing our job like every other person in society. They are selling different things to earn money like we do sell our bodies for period. We are also part of society and helping this dirty society to run smoothly. So never do like this again. I may not be there for you always to wait or hope she will be fine. Take care of yourself in this Jungle of Ocean", she said this very politely and left.

One mistake and I had a chance to know about my mother in all those years. I thought she was taking care of me but she was always there at that home. Maybe this is what motherhood means.

The next day morning, I and my mother sat outside our house. A random person was walking by and watching me lustfully. My mother observed that the person was watching me. Because of before day situation, she was very angry and shouted at him and asked him to stop there on the street. Everyone is watching on the street.

She stood up and walked towards him. While she was walking, she removed her jacket's two top hooks and pulled her jacket from the shoulders to the hands, exactly standing in front of him and taking a deep breath and releasing it like we do at intimate moments.

"You want to do something?", she asked him with intense expressions.

That uncle started shivering because everyone was watching on the road and his legs started dancing. And my mother took two steps forwards. He was afraid and fell backside. He stood up and ran from there without turning back.

My mother relaxed and said a word.

Motherf**k*r.

After all the situations that happened in my life, then I realized that the First moment in my life was not going to happen as of now because the person I wanted had rejected me. So, I need to wait for my First Moment. Maybe I can say that I am still a virgin because it relates to the heart, not the body.

Yes, I'm still a Virgin.

THE END

THANK YOU NOTE

And one last person, my friend's brother, my brother too, Rakesh Sanjay, who is the first reviewer of this book after completion of every chapter. Thank you for the support and feedback to think more clearly while writing.

Thank you, Rakesh Sanjay

by

Every letter from Naveen Miriyala

IndiePress

The best route your story can take.

To publish your own book, contact us.

We publish poetry collections, short story collections, novellas and novels.

contact@http://indiepress.in/

Instagram- indie_press